To Leahanne,

Every cloud has a silver lining. Shine!

Princeville:
The 500-Year Flood

Carole B Weatherford
2003

Carole Boston Weatherford
Weatherford
Illustrations by Douglas Alvord

 Coastal Carolina Press

Dedicated to the survivors.

And always, to Caresse and Jeffery.

"Didn't It Rain"

African-American spiritual

Oh, didn't it rain, children, didn't it rain

Didn't it rain, children, didn't it rain.

Didn't it rain, children, didn't it rain, children

Didn't it rain, children, didn't it rain.

*J*immy saw the weather warning flash across the TV screen. Hurricane Floyd was heading toward the North Carolina coast with one hundred thirty-five mile-an-hour winds.

In Princeville—a town with two stoplights, one school and no post office— Mama, Jimmy and Lavada packed their bags in case they had to flee the storm. Hurricane Dennis had struck North Carolina just two weeks earlier, and the ground was still soaked when Floyd hit later that same month. That night the wind howled at Lavada's window, a hard rain battered the roof and shadows of trees criss-crossed the wall.

"I'm scared," whined Lavada, running to her mother's bedroom. "Can I sleep with you?"

"Sure honey," said Mama, hugging Lavada.

"How can Jimmy sleep through the hurricane?" Lavada asked.

"Jimmy could sleep through an earthquake," Mama chuckled.

The winds eventually calmed. Princeville residents breathed sighs of relief and unpacked their suitcases. Mama, Jimmy and Lavada kneeled down and prayed. Their town beside the Tar River had been spared. Rain was all that remained of Hurricane Floyd.

The rain poured down for nearly two days, forcing people in lowlands to move to higher ground. By the time the sun began to shine, the Tar River was rising six to eight inches an hour.

At nightfall, more than one hundred people worked to sandbag the dike in hopes of holding back the floodwaters.

Shortly after midnight, Mayor Perkins climbed the levee and halted the work.

"The water will come three to five feet over the dike. We need everyone to get out."

Sirens and bullhorns blared. When Jimmy jumped out of bed, water was up to his ankles.

"Hurry!" Mama cried, grabbing her car keys. "There's no time to pack. Just put on your shoes and raincoats. We've got to get out of here!"

With a few belongings bundled in their arms, she and the children crossed the bridge to Tarboro to ride out the storm. They took shelter in the high school. Rows of cots filled the school gym. Jimmy and Lavada lay on cots.

"It's too noisy and crowded to sleep," said Lavada.

The next morning, Mama, Jimmy and Lavada returned to the bridge.

Motorboats sped down Princeville's Main Street, rescuing pets stranded on rooftops. "This flood could wash away every last memory," Mama whispered in disbelief.

She, Jimmy and Lavada lived on land that had been in their family for generations. In Princeville, families not only handed down land, but also passed along history and pride.

Years ago, on the front porch of a house that still stands, Mama's great-grand-pa John told her how Princeville began.

When the Civil War ended in 1865, ex-slaves left Tarboro, North Carolina plantations and settled near the Union Army camp on low, flat, swampy land on the Tar River's south shore. Eventually the Union troops departed, but the freed slaves stayed. They named their community Freedom Hill — after the little hill where Union soldiers had declared the slaves free. By 1885, the town had been granted a state charter and had changed its name to Princeville, for carpenter Turner Prince, a town founder. The town was the first in the South founded and governed by ex-slaves.

Over the years, floods came and went. In 1919, the Tar River rose to the railroad bridge. By 1923, though, the sun was once again shining on Princeville. Julius Rosenwald, the president of Sears, Roebuck, gave money to build a school for the town.

After the Army built the dike in 1965, the people of Princeville stopped worrying about floods. By the 1990s, they wanted to show off their historic town and planned to spruce up the old buildings. Hurricane Floyd put those plans on hold.

"When can we go home, Mama?" Lavada pleaded, clinging to a stuffed doll.

"I wish I knew," sighed Mama. They headed back to the high school gym.

Hungry babies fussed and children wove between rows of cots. Grownups traded worried glances. Some broke down and cried. Others recalled past floods.

"In 1924, floodwaters came up to my waist and in 1928, up to my knees," Mr. Peters told the children gathered 'round.

"The flood of 1940 was awful," said Miss Sampson.

"I'll never forget how fast the water rose last night," Lavada vowed.

"Me, neither," sighed Jimmy.

Later, the pastor came to the shelter. "If Noah's ark could survive forty days and forty nights of rain," he said, "we can make it through this."

"Amen," the crowd chanted.

Children from across the state and the country collected food, water, clothing, books, toys and money for families hit by the flood. Donations came by the truckload. Each day, more help arrived. The Red Cross set up a makeshift hospital. Under tents, volunteers cooked more than eight thousand meals a day.

Wearing donated hand-me-down clothes, Jimmy, Lavada and Mama lined up for dinner.

"Don't forget to say grace," Mama chided the children as they sat at a picnic table.

"What do we have to be thankful for?" Lavada griped.

"We've been living in a shelter for a week," Jimmy added, "and we don't even know whether we have a home to go back to."

"We're blessed to be alive," Mama reminded them.

Floodwaters rose twenty-three feet, as high as the traffic light. The town was underwater. Caskets floated out of graves and down the street.

"This is a nightmare!" said Jimmy.

As days flowed into weeks, the river returned to its banks, revealing the damage. Rushing waters had lifted, moved and cracked open houses, ruining furniture, clothing and family photos. In all, eight hundred-fifty homes were destroyed. Nearly two thousand people were left homeless.

Mama, Jimmy and Lavada went to their house to see if anything was worth saving. A water stain smudged the wall near the ceiling.

"Mud's everywhere!" Jimmy shouted.

"My room looks like a trash pile," Lavada whined.

"My new bike is ruined," cried Jimmy. "I only rode it once."

"This was Grandma's," said Mama, emptying mud and muck from an iron pot.

Princeville residents scattered. They moved out of the gym and into homes with relatives. Hundreds moved into travel trailers, many in an industrial park that they called New Life Park.

"This thing is too cramped for the three of us," Jimmy complained.

"I don't want to share a room with you, either," said Lavada.

"No bickering," Mama ordered. "Let's make the best of this."

Jimmy and Lavada were not only homeless but also school-less. They missed almost a month of classes because the flood wrecked the school building. The students were sent to other nearby schools. Lavada fretted about going to a new school, but her teacher and classmates made her feel welcome. In art class, she drew a picture of her family outside their flooded house. Above the house was a bright yellow sun along with the words, "We still have each other." Mama taped the picture to the trailer wall.

"That's nice," Jimmy mumbled, trying not to show he cared. Deep down inside, Jimmy missed his friends in the old neighborhood. Some nights, he lay awake wondering if his family would ever go home again.

Grownups wondered, too. Could Princeville be saved? People from all over urged Congress to lend aid.

The government gave the townspeople a tough choice. The government would either pay to rebuild the dike or buy out the destroyed homes and move people to higher ground. Princeville residents had to decide whether to stay or go.

"We could have drowned," one woman declared.

"We should take the money and run," a town leader grumbled.

"We can't turn our backs on the past," Mama insisted.

"I worked all my life to get what little I have," said Mr. Peters. "I'm too old to start over."

"This land is our heritage," said a preacher. "The waters tore down walls and uprooted trees but the flood didn't even crack the church's stained glass windows. That's got to mean something."

"Princeville is where we belong," blurted Jimmy.

"Hush," said Mama. "This is grownup talk."

The town's leaders voted to ask the Army to rebuild the dike.

President Bill Clinton formed a council to save Princeville.

"We must…help the people of Princeville who have bravely chosen to stay and rebuild," said the president.

At Thanksgiving, volunteers gave out free turkeys. For Christmas, Mama, Lavada and Jimmy strung popcorn to decorate their trailer. On New Year's Eve, they went to church.

"I've got a feeling everything's gonna be all right," the choir sang.

Five months after the flood, people trickled back to Princeville. Roger's Grocery was the first store to reopen. Lavada was glad.

"I hope you still have a sweet tooth," Mr. Barnes, the storekeeper, joked.

"I'll take a chocolate bar," said Lavada. She shared the candy with her brother.

"Tastes like old times," said Jimmy.

Mama beamed a smile as bright as a rainbow.

Within a year, Mama, Jimmy, Lavada and dozens of other residents returned to their Princeville homes. Teams of builders and volunteers had replaced moldy walls, warped floors and broken windows. With just a few donated furnishings, the room looked bare. Churches sent housewarming gifts of photo albums, cameras and handmade quilts.

On the first night home, Mama spread the quilt on the floor for an indoor picnic. The family began making new memories. Jimmy snapped his sister's picture.

"Princeville's coming back alive," said Lavada, "just like we knew it would."

Princeville: The 500-Year Flood
by Carole Boston Weatherford with illustrations by Douglas Alvord

Published by ◉ Coastal Carolina Press

www.coastalcarolinapress.org

First Edition

Text copyright ©2001 Carole Boston Weatherford
Illustrations copyright ©2001 by Douglas Alvord

Book design by Whitline Ink Incorporated

Printed in Canada

Applied for Library of Congress Cataloging-in-Publication Data

ISBN 1-928556-32-9